Text copyright © Penelope Lively 1992
Illustrations copyright © Frank Rodgers 1992

The right of Penelope Lively, author of this Work, and the
right of Frank Rodgers, illustrator of this work,
have been asserted to them in accordance with the Copyright,
Designs and Patents Act 1988

First published in the Puffin Post in Great Britain

This edition first published in Great Britain in 1992
by Simon & Schuster Young Books

Reprinted 1992 (twice) and 1993
Photoset in 16/23 Meridien by Goodfellow & Egan Ltd
Colour origination by Scantrans Pte Ltd

Printed and bound in Portugal by Ediçoes ASA

Simon & Schuster Young Books
Campus 400
Maylands Avenue
Hemel Hempstead HP2 7EZ

British Library Cataloguing in Publications Data available

ISBN 0 7500 1103 3
ISBN 0 7500 1104 1 (pb)

Penelope Lively

Judy and the
Martian

Illustrated by Frank Rodgers

SIMON & SCHUSTER
YOUNG BOOKS

Chapter One

It was the middle of the night when the rocket landed in the supermarket car park. The engine had failed. The hatch opened and the Martian peered out. A Martian, I should tell you, is about three feet high and has webbed feet, green skin and eyes on the ends of horns like a snail. This one, who was three hundred and twenty-seven years old, wore a red jersey.

He said, "Bother!" He had only passed his driving test the week before and was always losing his way. He was also an extremely nervous person, and felt the cold badly. He shivered. A car hooted and he scuttled behind a rubbish bin. Everything looked very strange and frightening.

It began to rain. He wrapped himself in a newspaper but the rain soon came through that. And then he saw that a sliding door into the back of the supermarket had been left a little bit open, just enough for him to wriggle through.

It was warmer inside, but just as frightening. There were large glass cases that hummed to themselves, and slippery floors, and piles and piles of brightly coloured tins and boxes. He couldn't imagine what it was all for. He curled up between two of the humming cases and went to sleep.

Chapter Two

He woke up to find everything brightly lit. He could hear people talking and walking about. He tucked himself as far out of sight as possible. Feet passed him, and silver things on wheels. Once, one with a baby in it stopped just by him. The baby leaned out and saw him and began to cry. "Ssh . . ." whispered the Martian. The baby continued to shriek until its mother moved the pram on.

The Martian couldn't think what he should do. He was hungry and he wanted to go home and the bright lights and loud noises in this place made him jump. He began to cry; tears trickled down his horns. He sniffed, loudly.

It was at this moment that a girl called Judy stopped right beside him. Her mother was hunting for fish fingers in the freezer and

Judy was pushing the trolley and also wishing she could go home; she hated shopping. She heard a peculiar fizzing noise come from the gap between the fish fingers freezer and the one beside it, and looked in.

Plenty of people, looking between two freezers in a supermarket and seeing a thing there like a three foot green snail with a red jersey on would scream. Or faint. I think I would. Not so Judy. She bent down for a closer look.

"Please don't tell anyone," said the Martian. "They might be unkind to me."

"Are you a boy or a girl?" asked Judy.

"I'm not sure. Does it matter?"

"Sometimes," said Judy, after a moment's thought. "It depends how you're feeling." She studied the Martian with care. "I think you're a boy. It's something about your eyes. Never mind. Some boys I quite like. How did you get here?"

"My rocket went wrong and I'd lost the map. Do you think you could help me get away?"

"I don't want to stay here," – the Martian's voice shook – "All these people make me nervous and the noise gives me a headache."

Judy looked round. Her mother had met a friend and was busy chatting. "Tell you what," she said. "Come home with us and I'll think of something."

"Will it be all right?" said the Martian doubtfully.

"I don't know," said Judy. "But let's try it anyway and see. Quick – get into the box."

Her mother had put a cardboard box into the trolley, ready to stack the shopping in. Judy looked round again – her mother was still chatting – grabbed the Martian, bundled him into the box and shut the flaps.

14

"I'm a bit squashed," said the Martian in a muffled voice. At that moment Judy's mother finished her chat and they were off to the meat counter.

When they got to the check-out Judy quickly grabbed another box and piled the shopping into that. Her mother, when she had found the right money and paid the girl at the till, was surprised they had enough to fill two boxes. "It's always more than you think," said Judy cheerfully. She picked up the box with the Martian in it and carried it to the car.

Chapter Three

At home, it was an easy matter to let him out while her mother was opening the door and whisk him round into the garage and behind the lawn-mower.

"Make yourself at home," said Judy. "I'll bring you some lunch when I can. Sorry I can't ask you into the house, but you know what mothers are . . ." The Martian said he quite understood – he had one himself. "I don't want to be a nuisance," he added humbly.

18

She brought him beefburger for lunch, which he liked, and sponge cake for tea, which he didn't, though he was too polite to say so. She also brought him some books in case he was bored, and before Judy's bed-time they played cards for a bit. The Martian was quite good at Snap, and even managed to win a couple of times. His horns went slightly pink when he was excited.

Judy and the Martian soon became fond of each other. "If a person's nice," said Judy, "it really doesn't matter what they look like." Which was perhaps not the most tactful thing in the world to say, though she meant well. "Thank you," said the Martian. "That's just what I've always felt myself." Truth to tell, he thought Judy was pretty odd-looking.

Chapter Four

Judy was worried that the Martian might be getting bored. It didn't seem any way to treat a visitor – hiding behind a lawn-mower in the garage all day.

"Tell you what," she said, "my great-aunt's coming over this evening while Mum and Dad are out. You could come into the house and watch telly. She's so short-sighted she'd never notice you aren't one of my ordinary friends."

The Martian was doubtful. "Are great-aunts fierce?"

"Not this one," said Judy.

So, that evening, Judy and the Martian sat
on the sofa and watched telly while Great-
Aunt Nora sat in the armchair and
interrupted. She asked the Martian how old
he was and what class he was in at school and
where he went for his holidays last year.

"Jupiter," said the Martian shyly.

Judy gave him a nudge. "He means
Cornwall, Auntie."

"That's nice," said Aunt Nora. She changed her reading glasses for her other glasses and peered over at the Martian. "Have you been ill, dear? You're not a very good colour, are you? I think your mother ought to be giving you a tonic."

"He's had chicken-pox," said Judy.

"Chicken-pox was spots when I was young," said Aunt Nora, "not anything like he's got."

"There are horrible new kinds of chicken-pox now," said Judy. Aunt Nora tutted and moved her chair a little further away.

The Martian quite enjoyed watching telly.
He said he thought they used to have
something like that where he came from back
in the old days. At nine o'clock, well before
Judy's parents came back, the Martian slipped
out to the garage again. Aunt Nora reported
to Judy's mum that Judy's friend was a nice
child, but a bit unhealthy-looking.

"Who was it?" asked Judy's mum. "Susie?
Ben?"

"Someone new I've got to know," said Judy. Which was perfectly true. No more questions were asked luckily.

On another day Judy managed to stay at home while her mother went to visit a friend. It was a sunny day and was a chance to get the Martian out in the garden for some fresh air. She bought them both an ice-lolly from the corner shop and they settled down at the end of the lawn for a game of Snap.

At which point, of course, the next door neighbour, Mrs Potter, came out to hang up her washing and looked over the fence. Judy hissed at the Martian to keep absolutely still. She went over to the fence and said good morning to Mrs Potter, specially politely.

Mrs Potter stared over the top of Judy's head. "My goodness, Judy, whatever is that? Sitting on the grass over there . . ."

"It's a garden gnome," said Judy promptly.

"Well!" said Mrs Potter. "I can't say I like the look of it much."

"Nor does Mum," said Judy. "She's sending it back. Don't say anything about it. She's a bit upset."

Mrs Potter nodded understandingly.

Chapter Five

Judy, you will have realized, was someone who was pretty quick off the mark. Never at a loss. Even so, it was clear that things could not go on like this for ever. And the Martian was getting more and more home-sick. Sometimes he sat behind the lawn-mower quietly sniffing for hours on end. Judy felt really sorry for him.

She told the Martian that she would go to the supermarket with her mother the next day and see if his rocket was still in the car park. The Martian brightened up. Then he said gloomily, "But even if it was, how would I get back to it?"

"I'll think of something," said Judy. "Don't worry."

But there was absolutely no sign of the
rocket in the supermarket car park. Judy had
a good look round while her mother was
inside. Come to think of it, a small red rocket
wasn't really the sort of thing that would have
been left to lie around for several days. The
question was – who had taken it and what
had they done with it?

She went into the supermarket to find her mother and help with the shopping.

When they got to the check-out her mother said, "Well! I see they've got something to amuse the toddlers now."

There, just by the exit, was the red rocket, mounted on a stand, sparkling with yellow lights and with a notice beside it saying TEN PENCE A RIDE.

A mother put ten pence in the slot, popped her baby in the rocket and the rocket jiggled about and flashed its lights. The baby beamed out through the plastic hatch. Judy stared. She hoped it wouldn't take off. But no – after a few minutes the rocket stopped jiggling, the mother lifted the baby out and put him in a push-chair.

As soon as she got home she rushed out to the garage to tell the Martian. He looked alarmed. "This is terrible! If they haven't got it properly fixed it could take off."

"They think it's just a toy," said Judy.

The Martian got very distressed. "It's this year's model. Goes faster than sound if you want it to, not that I've ever dared. Something dreadful could happen if they keep it there."

Judy thought of babies whizzing out of the supermarket faster than sound. She nodded. Quite true – you could upset a person for life, having that sort of thing happen to them at that age.

"What we have got to do," she said, "is get *you* into it."

Chapter Six

The next time Judy's mother was getting
ready to go shopping Judy popped into the
garage ahead of her, helped the Martian climb
into the back seat of the car and bundled him
up in her anorak.

When they got to the supermarket she tucked the whole bundle of anorak and Martian under her arm and carried it in after her mother. She was puffing and blowing with the weight. Her mother said, "Put your coat on – no need to carry it around like that."

"I'd be too hot," said Judy. One of the Martian's webbed feet was poking out. She tucked a sleeve round it.

"Suit yourself," said her mother.

The shopping seemed to take for ever that
morning. First her mother forgot the eggs and
had to go all the way back to the start to
collect them. Then she met a friend. Then she
couldn't decide what to have for supper. Judy
staggered along behind. The Martian seemed
heavier and heavier.

There was a long line at the check-out.
Judy could see the rocket flashing and
jiggling. A baby was having a ride on it. Judy
slipped away from her mother and stood near
them. Her mother was busy taking her
shopping out of the trolley for the check-out
lady. She looked up and said, "Judy! Don't go
wandering off!"

"Just watching the rocket, Mum," said
Judy.

The Martian poked one horn out from under the anorak and said, "I'm ever so nervous."

"So am I," said Judy. "The thing is, how're we going to get it off that stand they've put it on?"

The Martian peered a little further. "There are two screws. You'll have to undo them. Do you think you can?"

"I s'pect so," said Judy.

The rocket stopped jiggling. The mother lifted her baby out. Judy stepped forward and popped the Martian into the rocket, still wrapped up in the anorak. "Giving your little brother a turn?" said the baby's mother.

"That's right," said Judy. "He's mad about space travel." She bent down.

"I shouldn't touch those screws, dear," said the woman.

"I'm just checking that it's safe," said Judy sternly. Luckily the baby, who had caught sight of Martian's horns, was now howling. Its mother turned away.

"I've done them," hissed Judy. "Are you ready?"

"All systems go," said the Martian. "That's what you're supposed to say, isn't it?"

"I think so," said Judy. She whipped her
anorak off him and closed the hatch.
"Well . . . Bye, then. It's been ever so nice
having you."

"Thank *you*," said the Martian. "I'll send
you a postcard when I get back. "Bye . . ."

Judy stepped aside and put ten pence in the
slot. The rocket's lights flashed. It began to
jiggle around and . . .

Chapter Seven

. . .Well, they are still talking about it in the town where Judy lives. At least those who saw it happen are. Those who didn't say it was all imagination. But there are at least twenty people who saw a small red rocket go zooming three times round the supermarket and then out of the doors.

The local paper had a headline that said MYSTERY BABY TAKES OFF! And of course nobody ever reported a missing child. So after a while people lost interest, though the supermarket manager is still looking for that toy rocket he found in the car park. It had been very useful for amusing the toddlers.

After a couple of weeks Judy got a postcard of some very peculiar mountains, with stamps on the other side the like of which no-one had ever seen.

Look out for other exciting new titles in the **Storybooks** series.

The Birthday Phone
Toby Forward
Illustrated by Neil Reed

Helen isn't very happy with her birthday presents, so she decides to call the Birthday Fairy and complain. Two days later, a parcel arrives with the presents she really wanted! Who can the Birthday Fairy be?

Dreamy Daniel, Brainy Bert
Scoular Anderson

Daniel is a daydreamer and is always getting into trouble at school. But with the help of Bert, the class mouse, Daniel proves that he's just as capable as anyone else in the class!

Hopping Mad
Nick Warburton
Illustrated by Tony Blundell

Janey's daft little brother, Martin, is daft, clumsy and useless. But one day Janey discovers his one talent – he's brilliant at jumping around in a duvet cover. Why not enter Martin for the big pillow race at sports day?

The Saracen Maid
Leon Garfield
Illustrated by John Talbot

Young Gilbert Beckett is captured by pirates and sold to a rich Arab merchant. But the merchant's beautiful daughter falls in love with Gilbert and promises to help him escape...

You can buy all these books from your local bookshop, or they can be ordered direct from the publishers. For more information about Storybooks write to The Sales Department, Simon & Schuster Young Books, Campus 400, Maylands Avenue, Hemel Hempstead HP2 7EZ.